TALES OF
THE FAR NORTH

TALES OF
THE FAR NORTH

Eva Martin

pictures by László Gál

Dial Books / New York

First published in the United States 1986 by
Dial Books
2 Park Avenue
New York, New York 10016
Published in Canada 1984 by Douglas & McIntyre Ltd.
Text copyright © 1984 by Eva Martin
Illustrations copyright © 1984 by László Gál
Printed in Hong Kong by Everbest Printing Co.
First Edition
US
2 4 6 8 10 9 7 5 3 1

Library of Congress Cataloging-in-Publication Data
Martin, Eva. Tales of the Far North.
Summary: A collection of fairy tales adapted from
the French and English folklore tradition of Canada.
1. Fairy tales—Canada. [1. Fairy tales. 2. Folklore—Canada.]
I. Gál, László, ill.   II. Title.
PZ8.M4472Tal   1986   398.2'09719   85-46068
ISBN 0-8037-0319-8

To Alice Kane
and the Toronto School of Storytellers
E.M.

To Fred W.,
the first person in Canada who believed in me
L.G.

Contents

THE HEALING SPRING

ONCE upon a time, there were two brothers who lived in a little hut with their old mother. Jack was a bright boy and a hard worker, but Charlie was lazy and dreamt only of living the life of a gentleman. When he came of age, Charlie found a fine rich girl to marry, and they went to live in a grand house on the top of a hill.

Jack stayed home and looked after his old mother. He worked hard tending the fields and the few animals they owned. Times were difficult. After a while, in desperation, Jack went to visit Charlie in his grand house to ask for help.

"Do I know you?" Charlie asked. "Go away and tend to your own affairs. Don't let me see you here again."

Weeks later, Jack's old mother became very ill and Jack needed help. Once again, he trudged up to his brother's grand house on the hill.

"I don't have a mother," Charlie said, "and I don't know you, so be off."

Soon after that, Jack's old mother died. Because he had no money to have her buried, Jack had to do his own burying. So he fixed her up as best he could, slung her over his shoulder and set off down the road to the graveyard. After a while, he saw a farmer approaching with a herd of cattle. Jack moved over to the side of the road and stood his mother up beside him. The farmer passed by, but his cows would not budge an inch when they saw the dead woman standing there by the roadside. The farmer became angry and ordered the old woman to move away, but she stood as still and silent as stone. Three times the farmer asked Jack to take the old woman away, but still she didn't move at all. Finally, the farmer pulled a pistol from his pocket and shot at the old woman three times. Jack gave his mother a little nudge with his elbow and over she tumbled.

"Now look what you've done," cried Jack. "Look what you've done to my old mother."

The farmer was aghast. "Don't say anything about this to anybody. Take this herd of cattle in payment."

Jack agreed and the farmer went home. Then Jack buried his mother in the graveyard and drove the herd of cattle home to his own fields.

One day, Charlie was passing by Jack's fields and he saw the big herd of cattle. He wondered how his brother had come by such fine animals, so he stopped at the little hut and asked, "Whose cows are those over there in your fields?"

"They are mine," Jack replied.

"How did a poor boy like you come by such a fine herd of cows?" sneered Charlie.

"Our old mother died, so I sold her," said Jack.

"Why," said Charlie, "I didn't know you could sell a dead body!"

"Well, I did, and there are the cows to prove it."

Charlie was amazed. He wondered if the same thing would work for him. So he went home and killed his wife, put her in a cart and took her to the marketplace. There he was marching through the marketplace, pulling the cart behind him and shouting, "Dead body for sale! Dead body for sale!" It wasn't long before he was arrested and thrown in prison, where he stayed for many long years.

Jack tended his cattle and prospered. When Charlie finally got out of prison, he immediately set out for his brother's hut.

"It's all your fault, Jack. You told me you sold mother."

"I did sell Mother," said Jack, "but I didn't tell you to kill your wife. That's not my fault."

"Nevertheless," said Charlie, "I will get even with you."

One night, very late, Charlie crept into Jack's hut. He set a fire and burned Jack's eyes so he could not see. Then he carried his brother to the graveyard and dumped him amidst the rough stones and prowling beasts. He returned home, very pleased with himself.

When Jack came to the next day, he wondered where he was. He bumped against the rough stones and knew he must be in the graveyard. In those days, the birds and the beasts could talk, and Jack heard two wild cats who were prowling around near him say, "Did you know that in the far west corner of this graveyard there is a healing spring? Whoever drinks from this spring is cured of whatever is wrong with him."

Jack listened carefully and thought to himself, "I wonder if I can find that spring." On his hands and knees he pushed himself forward and groped about the ground in front of him and, after many long, hard hours, he plunged his hands into a spring of very cold water. He cupped his hands and sipped some of the water, and the pain in his eyes disappeared. After many mouthfuls of the magic water, he could see perfectly well again. "I must remember where this spring is," he said to himself. Then he returned home.

That night, Charlie noticed from his grand house on the hill that smoke was coming out of Jack's chimney and that there was a light in the window. He hastened down the hill to see what was going on. There was Jack, his eyes as bright and sparkling as ever.

Charlie was amazed. "I thought I had done you in for good!"

"Oh, no," replied Jack, "you haven't done me in at all."

"Sooner or later," Charlie said, "I will get even with you." And off he went home.

Jack thought it was time he got away from that place once and for all, so the next day he filled several small bottles with water from the healing spring and set off to seek his fortune. He walked and walked until he came to a fine city where a king lived in a beautiful castle. Everyone was gossiping about the king's daughter, how she was so terribly ill and soon would die. Doctors had come from miles around, but no one seemed able to help her.

Jack went up to the castle door and knocked. He was shown into the throne room where he said to the king, "I hear that somebody is very ill here. Perhaps I could help."

"Oh," said the king, "it is my daughter who is ill and soon will die. Many doctors have tried for months to help her, but none have done so."

"Perhaps I could try," said Jack.

"Well," said the king, "I don't think it will do much good, but it can't do any harm."

Jack was shown into the princess's room. The king and all of the doctors clustered outside the room and tried to peep through the keyhole. There lay the princess, pale and weak, stretched out on the bed with her eyes closed. Jack poured a little water from one of his bottles into a spoon and held it to her lips. As she sipped, the princess's eyes fluttered open. Jack gave her a little more water and soon she was able to sit up. After a few more spoonfuls, the princess began to talk.

"Listen," said one of the doctors outside the door. "I can hear her talking."

"Impossible," said the king.

Jack gave her the rest of the bottle of water and soon she got up and walked around the room.

The doctors were amazed. "I think she's walking around the room," they said.

"Bah!" said the king. "I don't believe it."

Jack unlocked the door and when they saw the princess alive and well, the doctors were so embarrassed that they ran away.

The king was delighted. "Marry my daughter and live here in the castle with us," he said, "for everything I have is yours."

So Jack and the princess were married, and they lived happily in the castle forever after.

THE PRINCESS OF TOMBOSO

ONCE upon a time, there was an old king who had three sons. There came a time when the king knew that he would soon die, and so he called his three sons together and said, "I will die soon. When I am gone, look behind the stable door. There you will find an old wooden bowl. Each of you must shake it, and whatever falls out of it will be your inheritance."

Soon after that the old king died. The three sons hardly waited for their father to be buried before they raced out to the stable. The eldest son, Jacques, grabbed the bowl and shook it. A purse fell out, and written on the purse were the words: "Whoever opens this purse will always find it filled with gold." When Jacques opened the purse, a hundred gold pieces tumbled out. The same thing happened a second time.

"Now I am rich!" Jacques shouted with glee.

Then the second brother, Jean, grabbed the bowl and shook it. A silver horn fell out. Written on it were the words: "Blow on one end and an army will appear to help you. Blow on the other and it will disappear."

Jean was also delighted, for he, too, would be rich and powerful.

Then it was time for Pierre, the youngest brother, to shake the bowl. A belt fell out. On it were the words: "I will take you wherever you wish to go."

"Hurrah," he said to his brothers. "My fortune is made, too! My magic belt will take me to visit the Princess of Tomboso. She is supposed to be as beautiful as the stars."

"You be careful," replied his brothers, "for she is very sly and will surely try to steal your belt away from you."

"Don't worry," said Pierre, "for I will never take off the belt. If she tries to steal it I will simply wish to be somewhere else."

So the young prince made himself presentable, put on the magic belt and wished to be in the princess's bedroom. The princess screamed and said, "Where did you come from? Did you drop out of the heavens?"

"No, princess," replied Pierre. "I am a man very much of this earth and I have come to pay you a visit."

"How is it possible for you to appear like that out of thin air?"

"It is really very simple," said the prince. "I am wearing a magic belt. It will take me wherever I wish to go."

"That's impossible. I don't believe you!"

"Very well then, princess. I will show you," and Pierre closed his eyes and wished to be outside the palace. He disappeared from sight, and returned a few minutes later.

"I really cannot believe this," said the princess. "May I look at the belt more closely?"

The prince took it off and handed it to the princess, who immediately clasped it around her waist and said, "I wish to be with my father." She fell into the throne room. "Quickly, father," she said, "a vagabond has entered my bedroom and tried to attack me."

The king was very angry, and gathering together a few soldiers, he went up to his daughter's bedroom. The soldiers grabbed Pierre and flung him out the window. He fell down and rolled head over heels until he landed by the side of the road more dead than alive.

For a day and a night he lay there unconscious. When he came to and remembered what had happened, he was very upset. "My brothers will kill me for sure if I return home without that belt." But he was so hungry that he dragged himself home.

When the two older princes saw their brother returning in the distance, his head hanging down dejectedly, they guessed what had happened. Each one grabbed a stick and beat it on the ground so Pierre would know what to expect when he finally arrived. They beat him about the shoulders and locked him up in a tiny room, threatening never to let him out again.

About a month later when his brothers brought him food to eat, Pierre said to Jacques, who owned the purse, "If you would lend me your purse, I could buy back my belt."

"What! You let the princess trick you out of a magic belt and now you want me to lend you my purse? Never!"

"Let me tell you my plan," said Pierre. "I will go to the palace door and ask to speak to the princess. When she sees how many coins I can pay her for the belt, she will certainly give it back to me."

Jacques handed over his purse, and shook his fist, "If you lose my purse, I will kill you!"

Pierre took the purse and set out for the palace of Tomboso where he asked to speak to the princess. She smiled when he was shown into her room. Before even saying hello, he demanded that she give him back his belt.

"What belt?" she asked. "I don't remember seeing you here with a belt!"

"Princess, I will give you as much money as you wish for the belt!"

"Hah!" she laughed. "A fellow like you couldn't possibly have that much money!"

"I could fill this whole room with gold coins."

"How can you say such a thing? Why, even my father could only cover the floor with coins. I don't believe you."

"For me, it is an easy matter. Whenever I open this purse, it is always filled with coins."

Again the princess smiled mysteriously. "How wonderful!" she said. Pierre reached into the purse and pulled out a handful of coins which he spilled onto the floor. He repeated this again and again.

Finally the princess said, "All right, I believe you. I will give you back your belt, but first let me open the purse to see if it will do the same thing for me." When the prince handed her the purse, she put her hand inside and then wished to be in the throne room with her father.

"Come quickly, father. That rascal has come back again to attack me." This time the king's soldiers grabbed Pierre and beat him until he was almost dead. Then they flung him out of the window into the ditch where he lay unconscious for four days. When he did not return home after all this time his brothers were sure he had lost the purse.

When Pierre came to he stumbled home to his brothers, a pitiful sight covered with mud and dead leaves. His brothers saw him coming and shouted a warning of the one hundred blows he would receive from each of their sticks.

They pushed him into the fireplace. "That is where you will sleep from now on, and you will have only bones to gnaw on for food."

After a month in that place, Pierre said to Jean, the brother who owned the silver horn, "If you lend me your horn, I would have enough soldiers to force the princess to give back the purse and the belt."

Jean was astounded. "Do you think I would allow you to take away my silver horn after what happened to the belt and the purse?"

"Listen," said Pierre, "I have thought of a plan. This time I will not go to the palace of Tomboso, so I will not even see the princess. I will blow the horn, a hundred thousand soldiers will appear, and I will lay siege to the entire city until the belt and the purse are returned." The plan seemed a sensible one, and Jean handed over the silver horn.

Pierre traveled to Tomboso. When he came near the city gates he blew a single blast on the silver horn, and a hundred thousand soldiers appeared.

"What is your wish, master?"

"I wish to lay siege to this city."

At that moment, the King of Tomboso happened to be driving around the city in his carriage with the princess, and when he passed by the city gates, he was surprised to see so many soldiers. Pierre approached the royal carriage and spoke to the princess. "Princess, if you do not return my belt and my purse I will lay siege to your city and you will all feel the point of my sword."

"Good heavens!" said the princess. "Of course I will return your belongings. But first of all, tell me how a person like you is able to call up such a large number of soldiers in so short a time?"

"For me, it is a simple matter. I have only to blow my silver horn and one hundred thousand men appear."

"I really don't believe that a person such as you could do such a thing."

"Very well, princess, I will show you." And taking the horn from his pocket, Pierre blew into the wide end. Not a soldier was to be seen. He blew into the other end, and one hundred thousand soldiers appeared again.

"Just a moment, young man, I am going to give you back your belongings." The princess unclasped the belt from her waist, and holding it and the purse in her hand, she approached Pierre. "Could I please blow the silver horn to see if it would work for me, too?"

Pierre handed the horn to the princess. She blew into the wide end and his troops disappeared. Then she blew into the other end and one hundred thousand new troops appeared. "What is your wish, your highness," they said.

"Take this man and batter him until he is dead." The soldiers beat Pierre into the ground and left him for dead.

For eight days and nights he lay there. When he became conscious again he realized he could not return to his brothers, so he resolved to die. Nearby there was a beautiful forest.

"Ah," he said, "I think I will crawl into that forest and

die." As he crawled through the forest he came upon an apple tree whose branches bore so much fruit that they touched the ground. Next to the apple tree was a plum tree whose branches also bent under the weight of so many plums.

"Before I die, I am going to feast on apples and plums," Pierre said to himself. He climbed up into the apple tree and began to eat. When he had eaten a great many apples, he began to feel rather strange. As he climbed down, he discovered that his nose hung right down to the ground. He was so startled that he fell out of the tree on top of his nose. "I am going to die bearing a six-foot nose," he moaned.

By rolling from side to side, Pierre maneuvered himself over to the plum tree and ate some plums. Soon he felt better, and his nose began to shrink. After eating more plums he ended up with the most beautifully shaped nose anyone had ever seen. For a long time he thought about the princess. Finally he said, "I do believe I see an end to my dilemma."

The next morning, Pierre cut some rushes and wove a little basket which he filled with apples. Then he went for a walk in Tomboso. A servant of the princess saw the basket of beautiful, freshly picked apples and ran to tell the princess. The princess ordered the servant to buy some for her.

Sitting in a large and comfortable armchair in her room, the princess ate several apples. She began to feel rather strange. When she got up she tripped over her nose. Horrified, she threw herself on the bed and hid her face in the pillows. When her father the king learned the princess was ill, he called for a doctor. The doctor examined the princess and took her pulse.

"This cannot be a serious illness, for she has no fever," he said.

The princess screamed from her pillows, "This doctor is no good, send for another one."

A succession of doctors appeared to examine the princess, but none were able to cure her. Pierre observed all of these comings and goings. Finally, dressed like a doctor, and carrying his basket on his arm, he went up to the castle to see if he could help the princess. He was taken to her bedside where she continued to hide her face in the pillows.

"Princess," he said, "I must see your tongue." She refused to show him her tongue. Taking her by the shoulders, he turned her over. "Oh, princess, you have a nose like an elephant," he exclaimed. "But don't worry. I will bring back some medicine that will make that nose disappear." He rushed out to the forest, filled his basket with plums and returned to the castle. He gave the princess a few plums to eat and her nose became a little shorter. Then he gave her an apple to eat and her nose grew so long that it rolled off the end of the bed.

"Princess," he said, "you have two or three things that don't belong to you. Give them to me. Otherwise, I cannot cure you."

"Oh, sir," she said, "I have only a little belt here that is worth nothing."

"Give it to me, princess. When you are cured I will give it

back to you." When he held the belt in his hands, Pierre gave the princess a few plums to eat. Her nose shrunk a few inches.

"Perhaps I should also give you this little purse," she said. After a few more plums, her nose felt much better.

"I have only one other thing, an old tin horn that is really worthless." And she gave it to Pierre.

When he held all three things in his hand, he gave the princess plums to eat until her nose was exactly one foot long. Then he removed his doctor's coat and cap and said, "Look at me princess. Remember? I am the one who you have treated so badly. You tricked me out of my most valuable possessions, so I will leave you something to remember me by. From now on, you will no longer be called the Princess of Tomboso, but the Princess with the Foot-Long-Nose."

And with that, Pierre clasped the belt around his waist and wished to be with his brothers. Jacques and Jean rejoiced when they saw the magic purse and silver horn, and the three brothers lived happily together for many long years.

THE THREE GOLDEN HAIRS

THERE was once an old man who had so many sons that he couldn't keep track of them all. The youngest son seemed very slow-witted and the old man was afraid that the poor fellow would not be able to look after himself.

One nice afternoon, the king happened to ride by. "That's a fine lot of sons you have there," he said.

The old man was very pleased. "Yes," he said, pointing to his youngest son, "and that fellow over there is going to marry your daughter."

"What! Marry my daughter!" The king was horrified, for the young man was not a fine prince, and besides, he had no money at all.

"Yes, he is going to marry your daughter," said the old man. "In fact, he is going to your castle to see her this afternoon. Would you please tell him who he should see when he gets there?"

The king was very upset, but he thought of a plan. So he wrote on a piece of paper, "Behead this man as soon as he arrives at the castle," and showed the note to the young man.

But alas, the young man was unable to read and did not know what was written there. The king sealed the note in an envelope and addressed it to the queen. The young man put it in his pocket and set off on his journey to the king's castle.

The young man traveled and traveled until it began to get dark. He was tired and hungry. In the distance he saw the red glow of a fire, which, when he came closer, he saw had been made by an old tramp who was cooking some stew.

The tramp invited the young man to sit down and share his meal. After the two men had eaten until they were almost bursting, the tramp asked, "Where are you off to?"

"I am going to the palace to marry the king's daughter," the young man replied.

The tramp grinned. "Who said you could do that? You are not a prince. You are just a poor fellow with no money or prospects in this world. What makes you think that you can marry the king's daughter?"

"Oh," said the young fellow, "I have a note from the king himself that says I am to marry his daughter."

"Let me see this note," said the tramp.

The young man pulled the note from his pocket, and the tramp saw that the king had written, "Behead this man as soon as he arrives at the castle." After the young man had curled up by the fire and was sleeping soundly, the tramp took the note and tore it up. On another piece of paper, in handwriting that looked very much like the king's, he wrote a different message that read, "As soon as this young man arrives at the castle he must marry my daughter." Sealing the note in an envelope, the tramp put it back into the young man's pocket and went to sleep, feeling very pleased with himself.

The next morning the young man said good-bye to the tramp and set off for the castle. When he finally arrived, he was ushered into the queen's chambers where he presented her with the note that the king had written. The young man didn't seem any different from any other fellow who might be courting her daughter. The queen showed the note to her daughter.

"This note is in the handwriting of your father, the king, and it says that you must marry this young fellow as soon as possible. So get busy and do it."

Soon after the young fellow and the princess went off to get married, the king arrived home. "What happened to the young man who came here wanting to marry our daughter?" he asked the queen.

"Oh, they are off getting married at this very minute."

"What!" roared the king. "Those were not the instructions I gave in my note. You were supposed to kill him right away. That fellow is not suitable to be my son-in-law. Let me see the note."

The queen gave him the note and the king saw that the handwriting looked like his. He was very angry and said, "That young man may be off marrying my daughter, but they shall not live together as man and wife. I shall give him an impossible task to perform."

When the young man and his bride returned to the castle, the king said, "You have married my daughter against my wishes. Before you can live with her as your wife you must prove that you are worthy of her. You must perform the following task — go to where the giant lives far across the river and bring to me the three golden hairs that grow on his back. Then you may live with my daughter as your wife."

It was a long journey to the giant's house, and after a few days of traveling, the young man stopped at a farmhouse to rest. While he was eating his supper, he told the farmer where he was going and why.

The farmer said, "If you reach the giant's house, and I doubt that you will, ask him a question for me. Why is it that there is a tree in my orchard that bears one kind of fruit on one side and a different kind of fruit on the other side?"

The young man promised to ask the giant this question.

He traveled on for a few more days until he came to another farmhouse where he was invited in to eat some supper. He told the farmer where he was going.

"That is not a very wise journey," the farmer said. "You will probably never return. But if you do arrive at the giant's house, could you ask him a question for me? When I was first married, my wife was kind and gentle, but now she is like a shrew, nagging and scolding all day long. What has caused her to change so?"

The young man promised to try to find the answer, and the next day he continued on his journey.

He traveled and traveled until he came to a very wide river. The giant's house was on the other side of the river, but there was no bridge to walk over and no boat to ferry him across. The young man sat on the river bank and wondered what he should do. Suddenly he saw something moving in the water. It came closer and closer and when it reached the river bank the young man realized that it was a ghost who had been swimming in the river.

"Hop on my back and I will take you across," said the ghost.

The young man hopped on the ghost's back and the ghost swam until they reached the other side of the river.

Then the ghost asked, "Should you talk to the giant and should he not eat you up, could you just ask him a question for me? Why must I continue to ferry people across this river? No one ever pays me or thanks me."

The young man promised to ask the giant.

So he went up to the giant's house and knocked on the door. The giant's wife answered.

"What are you doing here?" she asked. "If my man, the giant, sees you he will eat you up."

"Don't worry, I'll go away before he can do that," said the young man. He told the giant's wife about the three golden hairs and of the three questions he wished to ask. She told him to hide under the bed.

A little while later, the giant came home. "Fee, fi, fo, fum. I smell the blood of an Englishman," he called.

"No, you don't," said his wife. "I have been cooking stew all afternoon and that's what you smell."

The giant sat down and ate a huge supper and finally he went off to bed. When the giant was snoring, his wife reached over and plucked out one of the golden hairs from his back and dropped it beside the bed where the young man put it in a small sack he was carrying. The giant felt a pin prick and he leapt out of bed saying, "What has happened, woman?"

The giant's wife replied, "I have been dreaming about a

man who has a tree in his orchard that bears one kind of fruit on one side and a different kind of fruit on the other side."

"Well," said the giant, "if that man were to go and dig up the pot of gold that lies buried under the roots of the tree, then the tree would bear the same fruit all over." And he lay down and soon was snoring loudly.

After a while the giant's wife reached over and plucked out a second golden hair and dropped it beside the bed. This time it hurt a little more and the giant leapt out of bed saying, "What on earth are you doing, woman?"

"It's all right, man. I was dreaming of a man whose wife when they were first married was sweet and gentle and who has now turned into a shrew, scolding and nagging all the time."

"Hah," said the giant, "no wonder she has turned into a shrew. If her husband treated her as kindly as he did when they were first married, she would still be sweet and gentle." The giant went back to sleep.

In a little while when the giant was snoring, his wife plucked out the third golden hair. This time it hurt mightily.

The giant roared and kicked his wife and said, "What on earth are you doing?"

"Please don't beat me," she cried, "for I have been dreaming of a ghost who ferries people back and forth across a river. Nobody ever thanks him or pays him."

"The next time someone wishes to be ferried across the river, all that fellow needs to do is to dump that person into the water and let him drown. Then that fellow's ghost will have to ferry people across the river." The giant's wife heaved a sigh of relief and they both lay down and went to sleep.

The young man went down to the river bank with the three golden hairs in a sack and the answers to the three questions in his head.

"There you are," said the ghost. "I didn't expect to be seeing you again. Hop on my back and I will take you back across the river." So the ghost ferried the young man back to the other side of the river. "Now," said the ghost, "do you have the answer to my question?"

"Yes, indeed," said the young fellow. "The next time someone comes to be ferried across the river, dump him in the middle of the river and let him drown, and then his ghost will take your place as a ferryman."

The ghost was overjoyed.

The young man went on his way and soon he came to the farmer with the cranky wife.

"Here you are," said the farmer. "The giant didn't eat you up after all."

"No," said the young fellow, "and I have the answer to your question. Treat your wife as you did when you were first married and she will be as kind and gentle as she was then."

So the farmer smiled at his wife and spoke kindly to her, and she became pretty and sweet-tempered again.

The young fellow went on his way. At last he came to the farmer with the strange tree in his orchard.

"Do you have the answer to my question?" asked the farmer.

"Yes," replied the young man. "The giant said to go and

dig up the pot of gold that is buried under the roots of the tree. We are to divide the gold in half and then the tree will bear the same fruit all over."

So the farmer and the young man took a spade and dug out the pot of gold from under the tree. They divided the gold in half and put it in two sacks.

Then the farmer said, "Take my horse and cart to carry your gold in. I have enough money to buy as many horses and carts as I want."

The young fellow put the gold under the seat, climbed onto the cart and drove off to the king's palace. He gave the three golden hairs to the king.

The king was amazed. "Where did you get that bag of gold and the horse and cart?" he asked.

"The giant gave them to me," said the young man. "He was a fine fellow – kind and generous."

"Then," said the king, "lend me your horse and cart so I can go and see this giant, too."

"I'll even take you there," said the young fellow. He drove the king in the cart to the river bank. There was the ghost waiting to ferry the king across the river. The king jumped on his back. When they were halfway across the river, the ghost dumped the king into the water and left him to drown, while he climbed up the river bank and went on his way.

The young man drove back to his wife. With the bag of gold, they built a fine house for themselves, and lived there happily ever after.

LITTLE GOLDEN SUN
AND
LITTLE GOLDEN STAR

THERE was once a king who had two daughters. The older daughter was very beautiful, and honest as well. The younger daughter was beautiful too, but she had one grievous fault — she was very jealous, particularly of her older sister.

One day a handsome prince came to the castle. When he was introduced to the king's two daughters, he was enchanted by their beauty. He returned many times to the castle but couldn't quite make up his mind which daughter he wished to marry.

Finally the king said to him, "Come, now, my dear fellow. It is time that you made up your mind which of my daughters you are going to marry! You can't keep coming here forever, you know, without choosing one or the other."

"I am attracted to both daughters, for they are both very beautiful, particularly the young one."

"Then marry her," said the king.

"But," said the prince, "she has one nasty fault. She is very jealous."

"Then choose the older daughter," replied the king.

After a great deal of thought, the prince did indeed choose the older daughter to be his wife.

On the eve of the wedding, the princess's fairy godmother revealed to her a secret. "After a year of marriage, you will give birth to twins. They will be very beautiful. Both children will bear golden signs on their foreheads. The little boy will bear the mark of a golden sun, and the little girl the mark of a golden star. These are very lucky signs."

When the princess told this to the prince, he was over-joyed.

The prince and princess had not been married a year before war broke out in a distant land belonging to the prince, and he had to go off and lead his army. Several months later, the princess gave birth to twins, and it was just as the fairy godmother had foretold. On the forehead of the little boy was the mark of a golden sun, and on that of the little girl a golden star. The princess was very happy and wanted to share the news with her husband, the prince. When her younger sister saw the beautiful twins, she was more jealous than ever and offered to arrange for the news of the birth to be sent to the prince. But the message she sent read, "Your wife has given birth to two horrid monkeys that are hairy and squinty-eyed and have long claws on the end of their fingers."

The prince was furious. He shouted, "My wife has deceived me. These are not the beautiful children she told me she would bear." He summoned two soldiers and ordered, "Go to my home and destroy my wife and the two monsters she has borne."

When the princess received word that soldiers were coming to kill her and the two babies, she was puzzled. "Why would he want to do that?" she asked her fairy godmother.

"He believes you gave birth to two hideous monkeys," she said. "But you must not allow your children to be killed. Bundle them up and carry them away deep into the forest as quickly as you can. Don't stop running until they are safe."

The young woman, a baby in each arm, fled into the forest where she walked day after day, feeding on roots and berries, until one day she looked down from the mountains into a deep lake. As the sun set and it grew dark, she saw a light flickering on the other side of the lake. The princess walked around the lake towards the light and when it was very late, she came to what looked like an old ruined monastery. Moss was hanging from the beams.

She knocked on the door and an old man's voice cried, "Come in." When the old man saw the young woman carrying a child in each arm, he said, "And where might you be going?"

"I am fleeing from soldiers who wish to kill me and my children. Please give us shelter, for we are tired and have had very little to eat." Then she showed the old man her babies and the signs that marked their foreheads.

The old man marveled at their beauty. "I am sure they must be called Little Golden Sun and Little Golden Star," he said. Then he invited the young woman to rest for a few days, and he gave her venison broth so she could regain her strength.

Once again, the princess made preparations to leave. "Where will you go?" asked the old man.

"I do not know," she replied. "I only know that I must flee deeper and deeper into the forest before the soldiers find me."

"Walk in a north-westerly direction and after some time you will come to the home of my older brother," the old man said. "You will know him for he is older than I and has the longest beard you will ever have seen. He will shelter you for a while and you will be able to regain your strength."

And so the young woman resumed her journey. For many days she walked and walked in a north-westerly direction through the forest, stopping to rest only when her arms were so tired that she could no longer carry the children. They fed on roots and berries. Even after dark she groped her way forward, for she was afraid to remain in one place for too long.

Soon she came to the shore of another lake, and there she saw a hut so completely covered with moss that it blended into the forest.

She knocked on the door and after a few minutes a shaky voice called out, "Come in. Don't be afraid. I am a very old man and I will not hurt you."

The door opened and the princess saw the oldest man she had ever seen, with a beard that almost touched the ground.

"Come in and rest and I will give you some partridge broth."

"Thank you," she replied. "Let me lie by the warmth of your stove for a while."

"Not at all," said the old man. "You shall sleep on my bed."

The princess slept deeply and when she awoke the old man had prepared a fine meal.

"You are very kind," she said, "but I cannot stay here much longer, for soldiers are hunting for my children in order to kill them."

"Don't worry, my dear," said the old man, "for in my stable there is a horse which flies like the wind, and you shall escape on his back if the soldiers come."

So the princess rested for a few more days and then she prepared to continue on her journey. The old man advised her to continue walking through the forest in a north-westerly direction.

"Eventually you will come to the hut of our oldest brother. He lives in the remotest part of the forest and no soldier will ever find you there. Stay with him while your children grow up, and think about the direction your lives must take."

The young woman thanked the old man and set off on her journey. For several weeks she traveled in a north-westerly direction. The nights were dark and wild animals prowled about. Once she heard wolves howling, but she crouched close to a rock and sheltered the babies with her body. Then one evening she saw an ancient hut that blended into the forest so well that at first she did not see it. It was hung with moss and covered with lichen. She knocked on the door and a very, very old voice called out, "Come in."

"Good evening, sir," said the princess.

"Do come in," said the old man. "You have been traveling alone in the forest with such small babies. I know who your babies are."

"How do you know that?" asked the young woman.

"Your fairy godmother passed by here not long ago and she told me that a young woman carrying twins, one bearing the mark of a golden sun and the other the mark of a golden star, would be passing by soon and would need shelter. I will give you food and you shall stay here for as long as you desire."

So the princess and her babies spent several days with the old man, and the days turned into years. The children learned how to talk and the old man was delighted when they called him grandfather. Little Golden Sun and Little Golden Star grew and thrived in the hut in the forest.

After the children had celebrated their twelfth birthday, Little Golden Sun said, "Grandfather, I am twelve years old, but I feel much older than that."

"Yes," replied the old man. "You are as big and strong and intelligent as a fifteen-year-old, and I am going to tell you a secret. Many hundreds of miles away there is a beautiful garden high in the mountains that is filled with exotic birds and flowers. You must travel to that garden. I will lend you my horse. The garden is surrounded by a very high fence that only my horse can clear with one leap. In the garden you will find a dancing apple. Bring it home with you. It will be a dangerous and difficult task, but you have been protected from many dangers so far."

Then the old man led the horse out of the stable, and a sorry old nag it was. It was as lean as a skeleton and its feet were as long as tomorrow. "Now you see this beautiful horse," said the old man. "Climb on his back and clutch his mane for all you are worth and you will see what a fine steed he is."

"I will try, Grandfather," said Little Golden Sun.

"After the horse leaps over the fence," said the old man, "you will encounter many fierce animals — lions and tigers and unicorns. Don't be afraid. Clutch the horse's mane tightly and ride on to the apple tree that stands apart from all the other trees. And now, good-bye and good luck."

So Little Golden Sun jumped onto the horse's back, and suddenly the sorry old nag became transformed into a splendid white steed with a flowing mane. The boy set off on a trip that lasted a year and a day. His mother was very upset to see him go, and Little Golden Star wept for many days. The old man comforted them as best he could.

The magic horse leapt over mountains and rivers and lakes, its feet more often in the air than on the ground. One day they approached a field of flowers on top of a high mountain. As they came closer they saw that it was a garden surrounded by a very high fence. The horse gathered speed, cleared the fence with a bound and raced down the length of the garden. Fierce beasts howled and grunted. Then Little Golden Sun saw an apple tree set apart from all other trees. The horse raced by the tree, giving Little Golden Sun time to grab only one apple which he hid in his cloak. Then they bounded back over the fence and raced homeward.

One evening the boy finally arrived at the old man's door. Little Golden Star was weak from mourning the loss of her brother. The boy kissed his sister and hugged his mother, and they were so glad to see him that they both became strong again.

"Well done, my son," said the old man. "Rest a few days,

for there is yet another task before you. When you were in the garden, did you happen to notice a spring of clear water?"

"Yes, I did," replied the boy.

"Then, on your second trip to the garden, you must fill a little bottle with water from that singing spring. It was easy enough to grab the apple, but this time you must get off your horse amidst all those fierce animals that prowl around the spring. Do not be afraid, for you will be safe as long as you do not let go of the horse's mane. Fill the bottle as quickly as you can, leap back on your horse and leave the garden with haste."

Little Golden Sun rested for a few days, and then set out upon his second journey to bring home a bottle of singing water. Once again he was gone for a year and a day. He came to the garden and the horse leapt over the high fence, passed under the apple tree and galloped across the garden until it came to the spring of singing water. The water burbled and sang, while all around wild animals growled and lurked in the bushes.

With the bottle in his hand, Little Golden Sun got off the horse and, still clutching the horse's mane, he knelt down and filled the bottle. Then he leapt back on the horse which reared up on its hind legs to escape a pouncing tiger. They escaped from the tiger and raced home to the old man's hut.

This time, Little Golden Sun found his twin sister half dead from worry and his mother weak and ill. The old man was very pleased to see Little Golden Sun and the bottle of singing water.

"You have one final task to perform," he said. "Return again to the garden and bring back the Bird of Truth. When you enter the garden, the Bird of Truth will fly around you and try to rest on your shoulder. You must knock it out with one blow. If you do not succeed in doing this, the bird will dash you with its wing and turn you into a block of salt. Grab it firmly, knock it out, and then set it free, and it will follow you wherever you go."

Little Golden Sun rested for a few days and then once again he kissed his mother and his sister good-bye. He jumped on the magic horse and set out for the beautiful garden. Little Golden Star and her mother were very sad, for they feared that the boy would not return.

"He has successfully completed two tasks," said the old man, "and if he obeys my instructions he will return."

A year passed by, and Little Golden Star was weak and close to death and her mother was not much stronger.

The next evening, Little Golden Sun appeared on the magic horse with the Bird of Truth flapping along behind him.

"Come in quickly," said the old man, "for Little Golden Star and your mother are very weak."

Little Golden Sun held his sister in his arms and asked the old man to bring him some broth. After sipping the broth and seeing Little Golden Sun, Little Golden Star and her mother gained strength and consciousness.

"I see you brought back the Bird of Truth," said the old man.

"I did, indeed. It followed me all the way home."

When Little Golden Star and her mother regained their strength, the family began to think that the time had come to leave the old man and work out their destiny.

"It is time you started on your journey," said the old man. "Head for the nearest city. It will take about three days to arrive there. The dancing apple, the bottle of singing water and the Bird of Truth will help you."

The old man prepared bundles of food for them. "Good-bye and good luck," he said, and he waved for as long as they were in sight.

The princess and her children walked through the forest during the day and slept under the stars at night. Three days later, they came to a high hill and in the distance they saw smoke rising from the chimneys of a great city. On the outskirts of the city they came to a little house where they thought they could rest.

"Come in," invited the lady of the house.

"Good morning, ma'am. We wish to ask for food and shelter."

When the woman saw the two children and the mark on their foreheads, she was amazed. "I seem to remember a story about two such children who bore the same signs on their foreheads, but that was at least ten years ago. Come into my kitchen. I have just made a pot of stew and here is freshly baked bread."

While they ate, the old woman couldn't keep her eyes off the children, they were so beautiful.

"Tomorrow," she said, "there is going to be a festival in the city. Everyone will be there. Come with me."

So the next day they all went to the festival. There they entered a building that was brilliantly lit and had many beautifully decorated rooms. In the middle of one room there was a long table. Little Golden Sun placed on the table the dancing apple, the bottle of singing water and the Bird of Truth. When the guests saw these things they began to wonder to whom they belonged. Then the children turned around and people gasped when they saw the golden signs on the children's foreheads.

"Why don't you eat that apple, instead of leaving it on the table?" someone asked.

"I wouldn't eat this apple for all the money in the world," replied Little Golden Sun. "It is a dancing apple."

"A dancing apple! Come now! There is probably a spring under it that makes it move to and fro."

"Not at all. Just put your hand beneath it and you will see that there is no mechanical device moving the apple."

"And what is inside that bottle? Why don't you just drink it?"

"I would never drink the contents of that bottle, for it contains singing water."

"Singing water. You are a beautiful child, but you don't have many brains. Imagine, a dancing apple and singing water."

"And," said one guest, "do you think this bird should be sitting on the table?"

"Don't be afraid," said the boy, "for that is the Bird of Truth. In a little while it will tell you the truth."

All the guests laughed. Before long, there were a great

many people in the room. The guest of honor arrived, and on his arm was a beautiful young blond lady. This prince was the father of Little Golden Sun and Little Golden Star. Everyone bowed down when he entered the room.

When the prince saw Little Golden Sun and Little Golden Star, he remembered the prophecy of his wife, that she would give birth to twins, and the little boy would have a golden sun on his forehead, and the little girl a golden star. He wondered who these beautiful children were.

"Who are you?" he asked them.

"We come from the forest," they replied.

"And what are these things on the table?"

"We will show you. Apple," said the little boy, "I command you to dance."

And the apple began to dance to many different rhythms. Everyone marveled.

"Now that you have seen a dancing apple," said Little Golden Sun, "stay and listen to the singing water. Bottle, I command you to sing."

And the bottle sang a song. The prince was moved with wonder. Everyone watched him, for people remembered the rumor that he had tried to have his wife and children killed. The prince became uneasy. The band began to play a waltz and everyone danced. The prince danced with the beautiful blond lady. Suddenly, he bent and kissed his companion. At that moment the Bird of Truth shot forth like an arrow and struck the prince in the face.

The prince stopped. "This is a very fine bird, but it is very rough."

"It is no more than you deserve," replied the boy. "For this is the Bird of Truth and it knows everything that has happened in the past. Bird of Truth, tell these people all about the fine life of the prince, here."

The bird sat in front of the prince and said, "My beautiful prince, perhaps you may remember that in your youth you visited two beautiful princesses and you couldn't decide which one to marry. You married the older princess because she was not only beautiful but kind and true as well. She told you of her fairy godmother's prophecy, but when it seemed as though she had not fulfilled the prophecy, you tried to kill her. But she did not deceive you. Those two beautiful children are the proof. Your wife has wandered through the forest for years to protect those children. The children you believed to be dead are alive. You never once suspected the jealousy of the younger sister. It was she who sent the false message that your wife had given birth to two horrible monkeys. In reality she gave birth to the most beautiful children in the world, and she did fulfill her promise."

The prince was devastated. He threw himself at the feet of his wife, the princess, and begged for forgiveness. The celebration continued joyously for many hours after that, and they all lived happily ever after.

THE FAIRY CHILD

ALONG time ago, near a river in a valley where the hills rolled away into mountains, there lived an old man, Donald McNorman, and his wife, Janet. Nothing marred the peacefulness of this valley as Donald and his wife farmed the land. Birds sang sweetly all day long, the wind whistled through the pine trees, and the river burbled in its bed. Donald's hearth was always open and welcoming, for he was a man who liked to help people.

But all in all, Donald was not happy, for he had no son to inherit his land. But Donald's grandfather had always told him tales of the fairy folk, and Donald had faith that somehow the fairy folk would help him. Sure enough, one night they whispered in his ear that before long he would have a son. Donald's happiness knew no bounds. One evening he arrived home to find that his wife had given birth to a baby boy.

Great were the celebrations up and down the valley, and all went well, until one day when Donald and his wife were working in the fields, the little girl who was looking after the baby put the child to sleep and then went outside to play. When she went back in to check on the child, lo and behold, Donald's laughing baby boy had been replaced with a miserable, squalling infant.

In vain, Donald and his wife searched the entire valley for their baby, and they could only conclude that the fairies had stolen him away, and replaced him with one of their own.

Now, Donald's neighbors decided that perhaps the child belonged to the fairy queen. In the valley there was a huge rock that jutted out from the mountain foot, as flat as a table. The rock could be seen for miles around, and Donald's friends decided that if Donald were to place the sickly infant on the rock and leave it there all night, the fairy queen would hear her own child's cry, and would come and take it away, leaving Donald's own son behind.

So one night Donald took the squalling baby and left it on the rock. But the next morning when he went back, there was the same crying baby. He was very disappointed, but he brought the child home again and continued to treat it kindly. But after that, the child became more miserable than ever, and though it ate all the time, it remained sallow and thin.

Now one day a tailor arrived at the house to make Donald a grand new suit. Donald and his wife went out to harvest the crops in the fields, leaving the tailor in charge of the child. After a while, as the tailor sewed, the child raised itself on its elbow. It took from its sleeve a pipe and began to play the sweetest music the tailor had ever heard. The man was enchanted. He left off his sewing, put his needle in the cloth, and crossed his legs and listened.

A little while later, the door opened and twenty beautiful ladies dressed in green came dancing through the doorway. The tailor was so moved by the music that he got up and began to jig and reel about. When he reached out to swing one of the ladies, he found she was but a shadow. As he reeled about, another of the ladies gave him such a blow that he fell down, stunned. When he came to, the music had stopped, there were no ladies dancing, and he was sitting with his needle in his hand, and the cloth in his lap as though nothing had happened. The child was lying in its cradle. The tailor finished the suit quickly and left the house with great relief.

After this, the child was never still. It would get up in the middle of the night, sit by the fireside and play sad songs on its flute and sing. Donald became very restless and irritable, and threatened to punish the child, but his wife begged him not to lest the fairy queen should be angry.

One day, when Donald was preparing to go to the blacksmith's forge, the strange child asked him to bring back news of the blacksmith. Well, the only news that Donald could bring back was that the blacksmith's forge had burnt to the ground. When the child heard this, it screamed and screeched. It ran out the door, playing a mad tune on its pipe, and leapt over hill and dale, never to be seen again.

When Donald looked in the cradle, there was his own laughing baby boy. People from far and wide rejoiced with Donald. They had a feast and celebrated for days, while far off in the distance, they could hear the sad, strange music of a fairy pipe.

Jean-Pierre
and
The Old Witch

THERE was once a man whose wife was dead. He wanted to marry again, but no one would have either him or his only son, Jean-Pierre. Every morning and evening he beat the child within an inch of his life. The child was a pitiful sight – small, weak and pale.

One fine morning, Jean-Pierre finally decided to run away from home. He walked and walked until he came to a narrow forest path that led to a castle. There were no signs of life within the castle, and it seemed to be haunted. Jean-Pierre was very frightened and wanted to run for his life, but he could not find the path by which he had come. The only thing to do was to march up the stairs and knock on the door.

"Come in," a voice croaked.

Jean-Pierre opened the door and there stood an old, old woman before him who said, "Well, young man, where do you come from? You are the first person to knock on my door in a hundred years."

"My father beats me, so I ran away from home, and now I am lost."

"What are you going to do?"

"I do not know."

"I have no servants, and I could give you work here."

"I will do anything you ask."

"Then you will look after my black horse and my white horse. Listen carefully. Give the white horse only a little straw and some water. And take a stick and beat him as hard as you can. But take very good care of the black horse. Feed him hay and oats every morning and evening, and brush him every day."

"I will do everything you say," replied Jean-Pierre.

The old witch was very happy and showed Jean-Pierre all over the castle. They went through gardens, living rooms, kitchens and beautiful bedrooms. Wherever they went, it was as silent as death.

Then the old woman stopped before a door at the end of the hall and handed Jean-Pierre a bunch of keys saying, "You may explore everything in the castle except this room. This room is out of bounds. If you disregard my warning and enter it, you will regret it. Take my word for that."

"Don't worry, good woman, I would be too afraid to do that."

Then the old woman went away for several days without telling Jean-Pierre where she was going. Jean-Pierre took his bunch of keys and wandered about the castle as he pleased. One room was all in green, another was all in blue, and another all in red. Never had he seen such wealth or such beauty. But he wondered why there were no other people in the castle.

At midday, Jean-Pierre heard whinnying and went to the stable. He remembered what the old woman had told him about the black horse and the white horse. He gave the white horse a little straw and then grabbed a stick.

"Don't beat me," begged the white horse quietly.

"You can talk?"

"Yes, and if you treat me well, I will render you a great

service. Perhaps I will even save your life. As for that black horse over there, give him only a little straw to eat, and a good beating. He is not used to being ill used as I am."

So Jean-Pierre gave the white horse hay and oats and a bucket of clear water. But to the black horse he gave only straw, and he beat him well in the bargain. Then Jean-Pierre returned to the castle kitchen where he fed on the most incredible delicacies. Still there was no one around. After he had eaten, Jean-Pierre continued wandering about the castle.

By the following day he had seen everything except the room at the end of the hall. Jean-Pierre wondered what could be so unusual about the little room. So he found the right key on the ring, opened the door and went in. It was very dark. In the middle of the room was a deep and bottomless pit. A staircase wound its way down from the edge.

"This is very strange," thought Jean-Pierre. "I must find out what is at the bottom." He climbed down, down, down. In the darkness he heard a rushing waterfall. He put out his hand towards the sound and dipped his finger in the water. When he withdrew his finger it shone with pure gold.

"Oh," he sighed. "This is a fountain that turns everything into gold. Here am I, as poor as a grain of salt, yet this fountain is forbidden to me." He walked up the stairway, out of the room and locked the door. Then he tried to wash the gold off his finger, but it was there for good. So he bandaged his finger with white linen.

65

Finally the old witch returned, and she immediately noticed the bandaged finger of Jean-Pierre. "What happened to you?" she asked.

"Nothing much. I cut myself."

"Let me see it."

"It is nothing to worry about." But the witch grabbed his hand and ripped off the bandage.

When she saw Jean-Pierre's finger gleaming with gold, she cried, "Aha. You disobeyed my orders. You went into the forbidden room."

"It was a mistake! I wandered through all the other rooms and then without thinking I unlocked this door as I had all of the others."

"What did you see in that room?"

"Nothing much. I climbed down the staircase and something glittered. So I thrust my hand forward."

"Hmmm. You did not see much. You are very lucky. I will forgive you this time. But if you return there, you will surely die."

"Don't worry, good woman. Once in danger is enough."

The old woman did not stay home very long. A few days later she left, saying, "Feed and brush my black horse well. As for the white horse, treat him badly, as he deserves it." And then she went away. Once again, Jean-Pierre wandered through all the rooms. He had everything he wanted to eat and drink. But after a while he became bored. There was no one to talk to and everything was exactly the same morning and night. The forbidden room attracted him more than any other.

"I must find out the source of that golden spring." Taking the key, he opened the door. Down the staircase he went until he could hear a stream lapping against the bottom step. He leaned down to have a drink. His long curls fell into the water, and when he drew back, his hair shone a beautiful golden color.

"When the old woman sees me, she will kill me."

Jean-Pierre locked the door to the mysterious room and tried to wash the gold out of his hair. But no matter how hard he scrubbed, his curls shone as golden as the sun. How could he hide them? In a corner of the stable he found a piece of sheepskin that had been used as a doormat. He made a wig out of it which completely covered his golden hair.

At midday, Jean-Pierre went out to the stable to care for the horses. The white horse said to him, "My friend, now you are really in a fine fix. You must run away as quickly as possible, for the old witch will never forgive you for dipping your head in her secret pond."

Jean-Pierre decided to leave, but not before he had performed his regular duties. He fed the black horse and gave him a beating. Then the white horse called to him, "Give me a good helping of hay and oats, and brush me well, for I am going with you."

After the white horse had been cared for, he spoke again to Jean-Pierre, "Bridle me. In a corner of the stable you will find a comb and a little bottle. Bring them with you. They could be useful."

Jean-Pierre leapt on the horse's back, and they started

away quickly just as the old woman returned to the castle. The old witch soon saw through the trick Jean-Pierre had played on her.

"He will pay for this, the little rat!" She leapt onto the black horse and began to chase after the runaways, looming like a thundercloud behind them. But thanks to Jean-Pierre, the black horse was undernourished and weak and could not run as quickly as usual.

The white horse looked back. He saw the old witch coming closer and said, "Jean-Pierre, she is gaining on us."

"What should I do?"

"Take off my bridle and throw it behind you." Jean-Pierre did so, and the bridle instantly grew into a mountain of bridles blocking the way. The old witch and the black horse tried again and again to force their way through, but it was impossible. They had to go around the mountain. Jean-Pierre and the white horse raced quickly ahead.

After some time, the thundercloud reappeared and began to gain on them. "Throw back the comb," said the white horse. Jean-Pierre threw the comb behind him and it grew into a mountain of combs that blocked the road from one side to another. The old witch and the black horse had to force their way over all of those sharp points, and it took some time.

It began to grow dark. The white horse turned his head and saw the old witch approaching as fast as the wind. "If she catches up with us, we are both finished. Throw back the bottle, it is the only thing we have left."

Jean-Pierre threw the bottle behind him and it grew into

a mountain of bottles barring the road from the rising to the setting sun. The old witch tried to climb the mountain on her black horse, but they kept slipping and sliding. They almost reached the top when the black horse rolled over on his side and they both tumbled to the bottom. With a final screech, the old witch and the black horse returned home, their heads hanging dejectedly, as Jean-Pierre and the white horse flew away in the darkness to a new life.

GOLDENHAIR

IN A land far away, a homeless young man, Jean-Pierre by name, traveled on his white horse through the land. One day he came to a castle that had been built in an ancient forest. "It is the castle of a king," the white horse told Jean-Pierre.

"Do you think he would hire me?" said Jean-Pierre, a homely lad who wore a grey sheepskin wig on his head.

"You can only go and ask him."

Jean-Pierre went up and knocked on the castle door. The king himself answered the door, and when Jean-Pierre offered his services as a gardener, the king hired him, for a king can never have too many servants. Jean-Pierre was given a little hut at the edge of the garden to live in. It was near the stable so he could look after the white horse. Every day he fed the white horse hay and oats and brushed him from head to foot.

Now, the king had two daughters, of whom the youngest was the most beautiful. The window of her bedroom looked out onto the garden. Every day she carried meals to the new gardener. One fine morning she saw Jean-Pierre washing his face and his hair. She saw that under the sheepskin wig he had the most beautiful hair in the world, fine golden hair that shone in the light.

When she took him his dinner that day, she asked him, "Why do you wear that funny cap?"

"Beautiful princess, I am bald. People called me 'Little Baldy,' and that made me very angry."

"You are no more bald than I am," was all the princess said but she kept the little gardener's secret.

73

War broke out on all fronts. The neighboring king began to invade the kingdom. The call went out and everyone with strong feet and good eyes enlisted in the army. The white horse said to Jean-Pierre, "The king has gone to war, but he doesn't have enough soldiers, and he will lose. Do you feel like helping him?" Jean-Pierre was as brave as he was small, and he agreed. He took off his sheepskin wig and let his golden hair fall down to his shoulders. He put on a suit of white armor that he found in his horse's stall. And his enchanted horse became whiter than snow.

Jean-Pierre set off for the war at full speed. Like an arrow, he shot before his king's army. He passed close to the king and bowed deeply. Then he went on alone on the white horse to attack the army of the enemy king. Jean-Pierre and the white horse leaped one hundred feet in the air, sending off flashes of fire as they landed in front of the enemy king. Terrified by this splendid knight in white armor who attacked an entire army by himself, the enemy took flight.

Jean-Pierre returned to his king's battlefield where he again bowed deeply and then galloped off toward the castle and disappeared. The king returned to his castle, thinking, "I wonder who that golden-haired prince is. He is so strong and courageous that I won the battle, and not one of my soldiers was killed." When the youngest princess passed by he asked her, "Did you see a golden-haired prince dressed all in white pass by?"

"No, I saw no one more handsome than the little gardener," she replied.

"The gardener! Don't talk about him in the same breath!"

The next day, the princess took Jean-Pierre his dinner. She arrived before he had finished dressing, and again she saw his beautiful golden hair which shone like the rays of the rising sun. But she did not let him know that she had noticed it.

As Jean-Pierre was brushing the white horse, he heard that a second battle was about to begin. And the white horse declared, "We must help the king. Today we will wear red from head to toe."

At the appointed hour, there they were, completely attired in red. The horse's coat appeared a fiery red and the little gardener had taken off his wig. At full gallop Jean-Pierre crossed in front of his king's army, stopped briefly before the king and bowed deeply. Before the king had time to say a word, the red knight and horse had slipped away. The horse leaped two hundred feet in the air and came down in front of the enemy king, who was so astounded that he ordered his soldiers to retreat. The enchanted horse took Jean-Pierre back before his king and bowed deeply. But before the king could grab him he had disappeared in the direction of the castle.

Upon returning to his court, the king said to his youngest daughter, "I don't understand it. Once again a mysterious knight with long golden hair won the battle for me. But I do not know who he is. I tried to catch him when he returned, but he slipped away. He was even more handsome than the white knight."

75

"Not more handsome than my little gardener."

"Hold your tongue. It is not appropriate to speak of the red knight in the same breath as your 'little gardener.'"

The next morning, for a third time, the white horse asked Jean-Pierre to help the king. "Once again there is to be a great battle. Today we will attire ourselves completely in black to mark the death of our enemy king and the end of the war."

Both the horse and Jean-Pierre appeared in velvety black. Only Jean-Pierre's hair remained the richest, finest gold. Again the horse stopped in front of the king. Jean-Pierre bowed deeply, and then with his black sword clutched in his hand, he galloped ahead. Horse and rider leaped one thousand feet into the air, and landing in front of the enemy king, Jean-Pierre struck him down with the blade of his sword and routed his army so quickly that the sun was eclipsed by the dust it created.

The king was determined not to let this faithful knight slip away. "Cut him off," he cried. "We must catch him. I wish to know who he is."

This time the black knight did not take time to bow before his king, but as the horse leaped away the king hurled his lance and the point lodged in Jean-Pierre's thigh. Then the wounded man disappeared before anyone could discover who he was.

After he returned to his castle, the king plotted how he could discover who these three knights were. He decided to organize a tournament and invite all the knights for miles around to attend. Whoever brought him the point of his broken lance would have in marriage the princess of his choice from his two beautiful daughters.

Young men came from all corners of the kingdom bringing with them the ends of forks, pieces of ax, or points of a sickle, but none of these fitted the king's broken lance. The king dismissed them all. The only one who did not appear was the golden-haired knight.

One day, the white horse said to Jean-Pierre, "My old friend, the king is having a tournament today. Let us go to it dressed all in black."

They arrived just before the tournament started. They were all in black except for Jean-Pierre's golden hair which blew in the wind. The horse leaped into the air and came down in the middle of the tournament field. The king and his courtiers tried to grab him as he flew by, but he was as quick as lightning and disappeared like an arrow, leaving behind a trail of gold.

The king was very disappointed and said, "Tomorrow, there will be another tournament to which this knight is bound to come. He will not succeed again in passing under our noses like that."

Returning to the castle, Jean-Pierre led his horse to the stable, went back to the little hut and put on his sheepskin wig again. The beautiful princess saw him pass by and noticed that he limped, but she did not say a word.

The next morning the white horse said to Jean-Pierre, "Today there is to be another tournament. Let us dress in red." Together they set out, and the horse made a great leap which landed them in the middle of the tournament field.

Everyone had eyes only for the red knight with the golden hair flowing down to his shoulders. The king raised his arms and cried out joyously, "There he is. He won our second battle. Don't let him get away." The handsome knight in red paraded back and forth in front of the king, but just as he was about to be surrounded on all sides, the red horse leaped up and flew away through the air like a flaming arrow.

The king was very upset. "He is swifter than a fish in the sea. But tomorrow he will not make fun of us again like that."

Jean-Pierre tended the horse and changed back into his old clothes. He put on the sheepskin wig. The young princess who had only eyes for him noticed again that he limped, but she just smiled in a knowing way.

The next morning Jean-Pierre said to his horse, "Don't you think we have been playing tricks on the king for long enough?"

"There is only one tournament left. This last time we shall dress all in white for it is our best color."

Jean-Pierre sat on the horse radiating with light. His golden hair shone like the rays of the rising sun. Seeing them reappear on the tournament field, the king shouted, "There is the knight who won our first battle. Without him we would never have won the war. We must catch him this time."

However, the young knight was far too nimble to fall into any trap the king might set, and he escaped back to his garden. The king was very disheartened, and when he saw his two daughters he said, "My children, you have been very badly treated. Not one of those handsome knights came forward to ask for a princess's hand in marriage. You are destined to become old maids."

The king wandered dejectedly about his garden. The little gardener waited at the door of his hut for him to pass by.

"Look, Your Majesty," he said, "won't this iron piece fit exactly on the break in your lance?" The king turned around, astounded. How could a simple gardener have such pretensions? He said nothing but placed the iron piece against the break in his lance. He could not believe his eyes. He yelled at the top of his voice, "Come and see. The little gardener has found the iron piece that fits my lance."

"I found it while I was gardening."

"Never mind. I have given my word. Whoever found the broken end of my lance could choose a wife from between my two daughters. Now my little gardener, which one do you choose?"

Jean-Pierre took off his sheepskin wig and tossed it up to the castle ceiling. His golden hair fell in waves down to his shoulders. Everyone recognized in him the knight who had won the war. Without hesitation Jean-Pierre chose the younger, beautiful daughter to be his bride. People came from miles around to the wedding.

In the middle of the wedding feast, Jean-Pierre remembered his friend the white horse and went out to the stable to look after him. The white horse said, "Before we are separated forever, will you do me a favor?"

"Certainly, my white horse, for I owe you everything."

79

"Take the ax from that dark corner over there, and cut me in two. You will not regret it."

Although he was horrified, he could not possibly refuse. Jean-Pierre took the ax, closed his eyes, and brought it down on the white horse's head, cutting him into two pieces. A handsome prince emerged. The king was very pleased, for it meant that his older daughter would also be married. And the celebrations continued for many more days.

ST. NICHOLAS
AND
THE CHILDREN

ALONG time ago, deep in the forest far to the north, there lived two little children, a little boy named Pierre and a little girl named Estelle. Their parents died when they were very young, and their old grandmother was left to look after them. The grandmother was very poor and her hut was plain, but she did the best she could for them.

All went well in the summer, for there were berries to be picked and fresh eggs from the birds of the air and fish from the streams nearby, and they dug roots out of the earth. But when autumn came and the winds blew cold, the berries withered and fell, the birds flew south, the streams froze over and the ground was too hard to dig up roots. Soon there was nothing for the grandmother and the children to eat.

The grandmother was very tired from working so hard all summer and she became frail and weak. She knew that if she were to die the children would surely die, too. She could only become strong again if she had some broth made from fresh meat. The children worried to see their grandmother wasting away, so one day they decided to set out by themselves to find the nearest village where they could buy meat to make the broth.

For many hours they walked through the forest over the thick covering of snow that hid the ground. Pierre noticed that the holly-berries were blooming and that mistletoe hung from the trees. He was excited because he knew that St. Nicholas would soon be coming. Rabbits and other small animals hopped through the snow, and the chicka-dees chirped here and there.

A little while later the children came to a rough hut made of spruce boughs. There in the sunshine sat an old man with kind, twinkling blue eyes and a wrinkled, leathery face. He was carving willow whistles. The chips flew as he carved, and the pile of whistles grew at his feet. The children watched him for a long time before he noticed they were there.

Suddenly he looked up and saw them. "What are you two doing alone in the forest and so far from home?" he asked.

"We are looking for a village," they replied, "where we could buy meat to make broth for our grandmother who is very ill. She may die if we don't find meat to make some broth."

The old man gazed at them thoughtfully for a long time, and then he said, "In a village not far from here there is a butcher shop, but it is owned by a very wicked butcher. Often children venture into the shop to buy meat and they never come out."

Pierre and Estelle were very frightened by these words and they shivered at the thought of the wicked butcher.

The old man went on with his carving. "Perhaps I can help you," he said. "Take one of these willow whistles. They are magical. One blast from a child in danger will bring help right away. I am making them for St. Nicholas to deliver to all good children on Christmas Eve. Surely he would not mind if you received yours a little early. Go to the butcher's shop and when you get there, blow a long loud blast upon the whistle and St. Nicholas will come to help you."

Though the children were still very frightened, they took the whistle and went on their way. They walked and walked until it began to be dark, and as the sun set, the air became cold. At last they came to the village. And there before them was the butcher's shop. The light shining from the shop windows was warm and inviting. It didn't appear frightening at all. They crept up close and looked in the window. Long strings of sausages hung from the ceiling, there were plump turkeys ready to cook and bins of apples and pumpkins. The warm glow from the fireplace within was tempting and the children opened the door to go in.

But, just in time, they remembered the old man's words. Pierre blew a long sharp blast on the willow whistle so that St. Nicholas would know that there were children in danger. Then Pierre and Estelle entered the shop, and there was the butcher, pleased as punch to see them. Such a welcome he gave them. He sat them down by the fire and fed them until they were bursting. When the children were warm and comfortable, the butcher said, "Now, my friends, what brings you here?"

"We have come to buy meat to make our grandmother some broth, for she is very ill."

"Goodness," said the butcher. "I have lots of meat to sell."

Now the butcher was a very wicked man who worked with the local giant. The giant hunted and killed game for the butcher to sell in his shop and in return the butcher pickled little children as a delicacy for the giant to eat. The giant loved the sweet, delicate flesh of pickled children.

When the butcher looked at the two little ones sitting in his shop, he was overjoyed, although they were not as fat as he would have liked. The giant was due to come by at any moment.

Looking up, the butcher saw a string of onions hanging from the ceiling. "My little ones," he said, "surely you could use an onion or two for your grandmother's broth."

"That would be nice. She would be very pleased," they said.

Grabbing each child by the collar, the butcher lifted them both up to the ceiling so they could reach the onions hanging there. Then he lowered them and brought their heads together with such a crash that they were stunned. He shoved them head first into the brine of a large pickle barrel and slammed down the lid.

It wasn't long before the giant came to the butcher's shop. "Aha," roared the giant. "What a fine load of meat I've got for you tonight! And what, pray tell, do you have stored away for me?"

The butcher smiled smugly and removed the lid from the pickle barrel. He showed the giant the two children standing on their heads, pickling nicely. The giant smacked his lips and chortled with glee at the thought of the fine dainty morsels he would have to eat the next day, for he liked children to be well pickled.

Now St. Nicholas was a long ways off when he heard the long blast of the willow whistle. He was working very hard delivering presents to good little girls and boys. The snow was very deep, so it was some time before he reached the butcher shop. When he looked in the window, he saw the butcher and the giant smirking in a corner and he knew that all was not well. As he entered the shop, the butcher slammed the lid quickly on the pickle barrel, and the giant sat on it, trying to hide the barrel from the stranger.

"Yes, sir, what can I do for you?"

"I would like to buy a small piece of meat, perhaps from that barrel over there," he said, pointing to the barrel on which the giant was sitting.

"That barrel is empty," said the butcher, "but come with me into the back room and choose some meat from that barrel in the corner."

St. Nicholas looked into the barrel in the corner and said, "Yes, there is a small piece of meat I would like to have at the very bottom. Could you just reach in and get it out for me?"

So the butcher leaned over the barrel, but the meat was right at the bottom and hard to reach. He leaned further into the barrel and finally St. Nicholas grabbed the butcher by the heels and thrust him into the barrel and slammed down the lid. He held the lid down with a large stone, and that was the end of the wicked butcher.

When St. Nicholas went back into the shop, the giant was still sitting on the barrel, trying to hide it with his fat legs.

He said to the giant, "I would like a piece of meat from that hogshead barrel over there, but it is very tall. Could you get it out for me?"

The giant got off the pickle barrel and leaned over the

huge hogshead, for there was a little piece of meat in the far corner. As the giant leaned down, St. Nicholas grabbed a large shin bone that he found on the floor and brought it down on the giant's head. The giant lost his balance and fell into the hogshead. He was so big that the harder he struggled, the faster he stuck. St. Nicholas slammed the lid on the hogshead and that was the end of the wicked giant.

Then he went over to the pickle barrel and took off the lid. There he saw the two children standing on their heads, pickling in the brine. He lifted them out and warmed them with his hands and breathed magic upon them. Gradually, bit by bit, they came back to life.

St. Nicholas wrapped up a piece of meat for them, gave them a string of onions to carry and sent them home to their grandmother. They were just in time. They made some good broth and the grandmother became stronger and stronger, and they knew she would survive the winter.

And every winter after that, when the snow was deepest, the air coldest and when the night was at its darkest, the children kept the willow whistle close by so they could summon St. Nicholas whenever danger threatened.

BEAUTY AND THE BEAST

ONCE upon a time there was a young man who, when his father died, had no one left in the world. He decided that he must look for work. For three days he wandered about the country until he came at last to a village where there was a castle. He went up and knocked on the castle door.

The king himself answered. "What can I do for you, my fine fellow?" he asked.

"I am alone in the world," said the young man. "I have neither father nor mother nor sister nor brother, and I am looking for work. Do you have anything that needs to be done?"

The king thought for a moment. He looked the young man over and observed how fine and strong he was. "Yes," he said, "I could use a hard worker, as I have no sons of my own. I will adopt you and treat you like my own son. The pay will not be great, but when I die you will inherit my throne."

The young man was overjoyed at his good fortune, so he stayed at the castle, and he and the king became very fond of each other.

After several months had passed, the young prince was wandering one day through the castle grounds when he came upon a most beautiful garden. An iron fence surrounded the garden and the gate was locked. Through the fence the prince glimpsed the most rare and unusual flowers he had ever seen. He was just about to climb over the fence when a deep and fearful voice said, "Do not enter this garden or you will become an enchanted beast."

The prince looked around him but he could see no one. He climbed over the fence and gathered an armful of the beautiful flowers, for he knew that the king's birthday was near, and he wanted to give him a truly unusual gift. With the flowers in his arms, the prince was about to climb back over the fence when he saw standing before him a dreadful beast.

"You must return to this garden three times at sunset," said the beast, "and perform the task that is given you each time. Do not utter a sound, or show any fear, for if you do, you will become enchanted as I am."

The young prince, though he was very frightened, promised to return to the garden. He returned home, and when the king saw the rare and beautiful flowers that the prince presented to him, he was very much afraid.

"You have brought me a fine gift, but at what expense!" said the king, when he had heard the prince's story. "I know the garden where you found these flowers. When I was a young man, I, too, discovered that wonderful place and I was about to climb the fence when a frightful beast warned me that I would become enchanted and turn into a beast if I did so. Unlike you, I was afraid and returned home. You must keep your promise. Return at sunset and perform the task that is set for you."

At sunset, the prince once again approached the garden. The gate opened as if by magic. He entered but saw no one. Walking up the garden path, he soon came to a castle. In the castle he saw no one, but a rocking chair miraculously

92

appeared and gently rocked as if inviting him to sit in it. The prince sat in the chair and rocked. When the clock struck nine, three dreadful giants entered the room.

"Aha," they roared. "What have we here? Is it man or beast? Who are you?" The prince said nothing. "Hmmm. The cat must have your tongue." The prince uttered not a word.

"Tell us, do you like to play games? We do, and today we feel like having a game of football, but we don't have a ball. So you will be our football." The giants picked up the prince and, using him as a football, they kicked him around with great glee until he became unconscious. Then the giants grew bored and disappeared.

The beast entered the room. She was now disenchanted to the neck, and bore the head of a beautiful young woman. Taking a small jar of ointment, she soothed the prince's wounds until he began to regain consciousness, and then she left. The prince returned home and told the old king what had happened.

The following evening the prince returned to the garden at sunset. Once again the gate sprang open and the rocking chair was waiting for him in the castle. He sat down and at the stroke of nine, there appeared the same three horrible giants.

"Aha," they roared. "Here is this same young fellow. We didn't expect to see you again. What's your name?" The prince did not answer. "You're not going to talk to us, eh? Well, that was a good game of football we had last night.

Tonight we feel like playing baseball. We've brought our bats, and since we don't have a ball, you shall be our baseball."

Although he was very much afraid, the prince said not a word. The giants picked him up and they had a great time batting him about. Finally the prince lost consciousness and the giants went away.

Once again the beast appeared. Now she was disenchanted to her waist. Taking her bottle of ointment she spread salve on the prince's wounds until he began to regain consciousness. Then she disappeared.

The prince was astonished to find himself alone and he returned home and told the king all that had happened. "Who can be helping me?" he asked.

"Perhaps you will see tonight," said the old king, "for this will be the third and final test. Go back to the beast's garden and see what awaits you."

The prince returned to the beast's castle at sunset and sat in the rocking chair once more. When the clock struck nine, the three fearsome giants entered the room.

"Aha," they cried, "tonight we shall have the most fun of all. But at least tell us your name. Perhaps we won't want to play with you after all." The prince said not a word. "Huh, I guess you've lost your voice. Perhaps we can shake it out of you."

One of the giants picked up the prince by the heels and shook him up and down, but although he trembled with fear, the prince did not speak.

"We have just the thing for you," roared the giants. "All day long we have been digging a pit just for you. And so that you won't be bored, we have stuck sharp knives and razors into the sides of it. So here goes."

They flung the prince into the pit. By the time the prince reached the bottom, he was cut into a thousand pieces. When the prince remained silent, the giants disappeared.

What a difficult task the beast had before her. By now she was disenchanted to her legs. Gathering together all of the pieces of the prince, she joined them together with the ointment from her special bottle and at long last he opened his eyes. The prince saw standing before him the most beautiful princess that could ever be imagined. The beast was now completely disenchanted.

When the prince and princess re-entered the castle, they found a great feast awaiting them. In the middle of the celebration, an ancient fairy came into the room. She announced that the castle belonged to her and that the giants were her sons. As she had important business abroad, would the prince and princess look after the castle for her? The prince and princess were only too happy to agree.

"You may explore the castle to your heart's delight, but I forbid you to enter the room with the little green door," said the old woman.

She set off on her journey and for many days the prince and princess wandered happily through the castle, looking in all the rooms and exclaiming over the riches they found. Finally, one day, after they had seen everything there was to see, they remembered the room with the little green door.

"Surely it wouldn't hurt to take a little peek inside," they said.

On the ring of keys that the old woman had given them, they found a tiny key that fitted the little green door. When they opened the door and peeked in, they saw that the room was bare. However, when they tried to close the door, no matter how hard they pushed, it would not close.

A few days later, the old woman returned. "And how have you been occupying your time?" she asked.

"We have explored this castle from top to bottom," they replied.

As the old woman looked about her, she saw that the little green door was open. She was very angry. "You disobeyed my orders," she said. "Therefore you will have to pay for your mistake. You will both wander for a year and a day around the shores of the Gray Sea. You will travel in that direction," she said to the prince and sent him off. "And you," she said to the princess, "will travel in the opposite direction. Here are six pairs of steel shoes. When they are worn through, you will meet your prince again. And here are three beautiful dresses — one as beautiful as the sun, one as beautiful as the moon, and one as beautiful as the stars. Take them with you."

With tears in her heart, the princess departed on her journey. She did everything she could to wear out her steel shoes. She kicked and scuffed them against rocks and tree roots, and slid down the sides of mountains. Finally, after a year and a day, the last pair of steel shoes was worn out.

After a year and a day, the wandering prince came to a magnificent castle and hired himself out to the king. Unknowingly, the princess arrived at the same castle and obtained work looking after the sheep. As a shepherdess, she slept in a little hut in the fields close to her sheep. One morning she noticed a great flurry of activity around the castle. She asked the little boy who brought her meals what was happening. He replied that a few days earlier, a young man had come to work at the castle. The king's daughter had fallen in love with him, so the king had decided that they should marry. The princess thought to herself that perhaps this was her prince.

The next morning when she arose she put on the dress that was as beautiful as the sun. When the king's daughter looked out the window and saw a shepherd girl parading about the fields in such a beautiful dress, she called to the king, "Father, why should a mere shepherdess wear such a dress to look after the sheep. I want a dress exactly like that. After all, I am a king's daughter."

The king searched high and low through village and town but could not find a similar dress. Finally he had no choice but to go to the shepherdess and ask her to sell him the dress.

"This dress is neither for sale nor to be given away. It must be earned," the shepherdess replied.

"What do you mean?" asked the king.

"Allow me to spend the night with the young man who is going to marry your daughter and the dress is yours."

The king agreed. But before the shepherdess arrived, he filled two glasses with wine and put a sleeping potion in each one. When the young man and the shepherdess met, they each sipped some wine and fell asleep instantly.

The next morning the shepherdess returned to her hut and put on the dress that was as beautiful as the moon. When the king's daughter saw this dress, she was filled with desire to own it as well.

The king went again to the shepherdess to ask her to give him the dress.

"Oh, no," replied the shepherdess. "This dress is not to give or sell, but must be earned. Allow me to spend a second night with the young man who is to marry your daughter. Then the dress will be yours."

The king agreed and once again he filled two glasses with wine and placed a sleeping potion in each. Unfortunately, the young man sipped the wine immediately and fell asleep. But the shepherdess threw hers away. She wrote a note to the sleeping young man, which said, "I will come again tomorrow night. Do not drink any wine, for it is I whom you disenchanted in the beast's castle. This will be our last chance to remain together forever." She folded the paper and put it in his pocket.

The next morning, the young man discovered the note and read what the shepherdess had written.

The shepherdess returned to her hut and put on the dress that was as beautiful as the stars. The king's daughter, seeing the shepherdess's beautiful gown from her window, was furious.

"Father, how dare a shepherdess wear a dress that is fit only to be worn by a king's daughter. I must have it."

The king approached the shepherdess hoping to buy the beautiful dress.

"This dress is neither to sell nor to give, but must be earned," she replied. "Allow me to spend the night one more time with the young man who is to marry your daughter, and you shall have this beautiful dress."

For a third time, the king agreed, but this time neither the shepherdess nor the young man drank their wine. They waited until everyone was fast asleep and then they talked for a long time. They were overjoyed to discover that they were the same prince and princess who had met in the beast's garden and who had traveled around the shores of the Gray Sea before reuniting. They vowed to marry.

The next morning, the prince and princess told their story to the king. The king's daughter was so happy to own the dress that was as beautiful as the stars, that she didn't mind not marrying the young man. The king agreed to marry the prince and princess and a splendid wedding feast was arranged. People came from miles around. In the middle of the feast, a coach arrived pulled by four magnificent black horses. Inside was the ancient fairy who had sent them on their journey.

The prince and princess traveled back with the old fairy to her castle, where she said, "You have done well. You have completed your journey. Stay with me and all that I have will be yours."

A few months later the old fairy died, and the prince and princess lived happily in her castle for the rest of their lives.

TI-JEAN AND THE UNICORN

TI-JEAN was such a lazy fellow. He loved to sit in front of his hut every morning and snooze in the sunshine. In the afternoon he would stretch out in the fragrant meadow grasses, or curl up in a haystack and go to sleep. But every afternoon when the sun was hottest, big blue flies came swarming and buzzing around Ti-Jean's head, and they would not let him sleep. He tossed and he turned, flinging his arms about, but they still kept buzzing around his head.

Finally, Ti-Jean became angry. "All right, you flies," he said, "I am going to give you something to eat. Don't go away." He went into his hut and found a board, some brown sugar, a loaf of bread and some milk. He took them outside and spread the brown sugar and the bread on the board and stirred in the milk.

"There now, you flies," he said. "Come and eat. It's all for you." In no time at all the flies had swarmed down on the food and were greedily eating.

Ti-Jean rolled up his shirtsleeve and spat on his hand. He brought his hand down, bang!, on the board, killing one thousand flies, and a second time, bang!, killing five hundred flies. Ti-Jean was very pleased with himself. He took the board and made it into a sign, and on the sign he wrote, "Ti-Jean killed one thousand with the first blow and five hundred with the second." He put up the sign by the roadside and then he curled up in the haystack, where he slept soundly.

Not long after, the king came riding by in his carriage. He stopped when he saw the sign and read, "Ti-Jean killed

103

one thousand with the first blow and five hundred with the second." The king was amazed, and he said to his coachman, "Go and wake up that fellow Ti-Jean and bring him here. I want to talk to him."

"Nothing doing," replied the coachman. "Do you think I want to be killed?"

"Just tell him that the king wishes to talk to him."

Very reluctantly the coachman approached the haystack. "Er, excuse me, er, Mr. Ti-Jean, sir." There was no answer but a snore. The coachman went right up to where Ti-Jean lay curled up in the haystack and shook him, until Ti-Jean opened one eye and said, "What do you want?"

"His Majesty the king is waiting over there in his carriage, and he would like to talk to you."

Ti-Jean jumped up, shook the hay out of his clothes and approached the king. "Good morning, Your Majesty," he said, bowing low.

"Tell me," said the king, "is what this sign says true? Did you really kill one thousand with the first blow and five hundred with the second?"

"Yes, indeed, it is true," replied Ti-Jean.

"Then you are just the fellow to come and work for me. I have some work that badly needs to be done."

"What sort of work do you want done?" asked Ti-Jean.

"Many monsters roam in my forest, but the most dangerous is the unicorn, for it kills man and beast alike. Get rid of it for me."

"Very well," said Ti-Jean, "but first of all I will need something to eat."

The king rummaged about in a basket and pulled out several packets of sandwiches.

When Ti-Jean had eaten his fill, he set off down the path into the forest. "Follow that path through the forest," called the king. "It leads to an old ruined church where the unicorn lives."

Ti-Jean strutted down the path feeling very full of himself. The path twisted and turned through dense, tangled underbrush. It grew darker and darker, and as the trees became larger and larger, Ti-Jean began to feel smaller and smaller. Suddenly, from behind a huge rock appeared the unicorn, with eyes as big as fists. It pawed the ground impatiently and whirled its horn around in the air.

Ti-Jean was so frightened that he couldn't run. He just kept on walking straight ahead through the forest. The startled unicorn followed along right behind Ti-Jean. When Ti-Jean saw the ruined church ahead of him, he walked right on into the church and hid behind the door. The unicorn, following on the heels of Ti-Jean, went into the church, too. Ti-Jean had just enough time to pop out from behind the door and slam it shut. The unicorn was now a prisoner in the church and was very angry. Ti-Jean could hear it racing around the church, banging the walls with its horn. Ti-Jean climbed up on the ruined stone wall and looked down. There was the unicorn with its huge eyes glowing in the dark, whirling its horn round and round.

Ti-Jean returned to the king.

"Well, Ti-Jean," said the king. "I didn't expect you back so soon. Your orders were to kill the unicorn."

"I have got rid of it for you, Your Majesty," said Ti-Jean.

"That's impossible. I don't believe you!"

"It is true. I grabbed it by the tail and flung it into the old church. Come along with me and I will show you."

Ti-Jean and the king proceeded through the forest until they came to the old ruined church. As they approached, they could hear a great noise coming from within. It was the unicorn stamping and banging and bellowing with fury. The king was impressed. In fact, he was very frightened.

"I'll open the door so you can see it," said Ti-Jean.

"No, no, don't do that," said the king. "I don't think that is a good idea."

"Don't worry, Your Majesty. I will just grab it by the tail and fling it back in again."

"No, Ti-Jean, I really don't think that would be wise," said the king.

"Well, you should at least see the unicorn," said Ti-Jean.

So they climbed up on the old ruined stone wall and looked down. There, sure enough, was the unicorn with its eyes as large as fists glowing in the dark, stamping the ground in anger, and whirling its horn around. They climbed down from the wall and the king returned to his castle, pleased that his forest was safe from the unicorn. Ti-Jean returned to his haystack and curled up for a long, uninterrupted snooze, and the unicorn lived in the old ruined church until it died.

Ti-Jean Brings Home
The Moon

THE king told everyone far and wide what a fine, brave fellow Ti-Jean was — a man who could kill one thousand with the first blow and five hundred with the second, and who had grabbed the unicorn by the tail and flung him into the old church. The faithful coachman who drove the king wherever he wanted to go in his carriage became very jealous of that fellow, Ti-Jean.

One day he said to the king, "That Ti-Jean boasts so much, that one day he will burst. Do you know what he is telling everybody now? He says that he is not afraid to go to the giant's house in the forest and bring back the seven league boots that the giant keeps chained under his bed, with a chain that is three inches thick."

"Well, if he says he can do that, then he must do it." And the king called Ti-Jean to appear before him. "Ti-Jean," he asked, "is it true that you are telling everyone that you can bring back the seven league boots that the giant keeps chained under his bed?"

"No," said Ti-Jean, "I did not say that, Your Majesty. But if you wish me to do it, I will try. But I will need two things to take with me."

"What will you need?"

"I will need an invisible coat and a file that cuts through one inch of steel with each scrape."

It took the king some time to find those things, but finally he handed them over to Ti-Jean.

Ti-Jean put on the invisible coat, thrust the file in his pocket, and set off through the forest.

The giant lived in the heart of the forest, far beyond the

old ruined church where the unicorn had been captured. Ti-Jean traveled and traveled until finally he came to the giant's house. He peeked in the window. The giant and his wife and little girl were having their supper. The little girl was sitting on the floor, but even so, she was so tall that she towered over Ti-Jean. Still wearing the invisible coat, Ti-Jean crept into the giant's house, found the bedroom and crawled under the bed. There were the seven league boots anchored to the floor with a three-inch chain.

When supper was finished, the giant had a long smoke and finally they all went to bed. Soon they were snoring loudly. Carefully, Ti-Jean took the file from his pocket, grasped the chain and made one scrape. The sparks flew and the noise was so great that the giant jumped out of bed, saying, "Hey, hey, someone is in this room. There is someone under that bed, I know there is!"

"Go back to bed, you lout," said his wife. "You were only dreaming."

"I know there is someone under this bed and I am going to get down and see who it is," roared the giant.

The giant's wife gave him such a cuff on the head, saying, "Go to sleep, you old fool," that he finally lay down, and soon they were all snoring again.

Ti-Jean put a boot on each foot. Then he took the file and quickly made two scrapes. The chain lay in pieces. Wearing the seven league boots, Ti-Jean leapt out the door and was halfway through the forest, traveling seven leagues at each step, leaving the giant roaring in the doorway, shaking his fist.

The king was very pleased to receive the seven league boots. They would come in handy when he went striding vigorously throughout the countryside. But the coachman was more jealous than ever, because everyone was talking about Ti-Jean's exploits.

One day, the coachman said to the king, "Your Majesty, do you know what that fellow Ti-Jean is saying now? He is telling everyone that he could go back to the giant's house and bring back the moon that the giant keeps there."

"Well," said the king, "if he said that then he must do it." He called Ti-Jean before him and said, "Ti-Jean, is it true that you are telling people that you are not afraid to go to the giant's house and bring back the moon that he keeps hanging from the ceiling?"

"No," replied Ti-Jean, "I did not say that at all. But if you want me to, I will try to do it. But I will need something to take with me."

"What will you need this time? I hope it will not be too difficult to find."

"This time I will only need a five-pound bag of salt," Ti-Jean replied.

"That's easy," said the king, and he provided the five-pound bag of salt. Ti-Jean put on the invisible coat again and away he went through the forest to the giant's house. When he arrived there, he peeked in the door, and there was the giant bending over an enormous pot, making soup.

Ti-Jean waited until the giant turned away to cut up the vegetables for the soup. Then he crept into the house, climbed up on a stool and dumped the five-pound bag of salt into the soup. Then he hid behind the door. The giant finished cutting up the vegetables and threw them into the soup and stirred and stirred until the soup was done. Then he and his wife sat at the table and began to drink the soup.

Something was not quite right about the soup. The giant began to hiccup. "Wife, hiccup," he said. "Why did you put so much salt in the soup, hiccup?"

"I didn't put any salt in the soup," said his wife.

"Well, hiccup, there is certainly something wrong with it, hiccup." Then he said to his little girl, "Go out to the well in the yard and bring me a barrel of water so I can quench my thirst and get rid of these hiccups."

"Oh, no," cried the little giant girl. "I can't do that. I am too afraid. It is too dark out there in the yard."

"Then take down the moon from its hook in the ceiling and it will light your way to the well."

The giant's daughter got down the moon from its hook and held it in front of her so it would light a path to the well. Ti-Jean, still wearing the invisible coat, crept out the door and followed her. When she was well across the yard, he grabbed the moon from her and was halfway through the forest before the giant family realized what had happened.

The king was very pleased to receive the moon. He hung it up in a tree where everyone in the countryside could see it. And Ti-Jean was pleased, too.

TI-JEAN AND THE WHITE CAT

ONCE upon a time, in a kingdom far away, there lived an old king who had neither sons nor daughters to inherit his crown. So he invited all the fine young men of the land to come to his castle so he could look them over and decide who was best suited to be the next king. And of all the young men who came, there were three who were so perfect that the king couldn't choose from among them. One of them was that rascal, Ti-Jean. The king looked over the three young men, scratched his beard, and thought and thought. Finally he said, "Off you go down that road, you young fellows. Whoever brings back the finest horse in the land will be the next king."

The three fellows set off eagerly down the road. After a while they came to a place where the road divided into three. Each fellow chose a different road to travel down. Ti-Jean sauntered on and on until he came to the end of the road. There he found a little path that led through the forest. He walked down the path until he came to a thatched cottage. There in the yard of the cottage were a white cat and four toads. They were all helping to fill a tub with water. When the tub was filled, the white cat jumped into the water. After a while, out of the tub came the most beautiful princess that Ti-Jean had ever seen.

The princess looked at Ti-Jean and said, "What are you looking for?"

"I'm looking for a horse, that's what I'm looking for. The king promised that whoever brings back the most beautiful horse in the land will inherit his crown."

"Well, tomorrow morning I will turn into a white cat again," the princess said. "When I do, go into the stable and take away the ugliest toad that you can find there. Take him back to the king's castle and the next morning, when you lead him before the king, he will be the finest horse you have ever seen."

The next morning, Ti-Jean went into the stable and selected the ugliest toad he could find. You can imagine how his two rivals laughed when he met them at the crossroads.

"You'd better be careful," they said, "for when the king sees you riding that toad, he may think you're making fun of him and have you put to death."

Ti-Jean just smiled. He rode on his toad and whipped him along with a piece of string. When the three young men arrived at the king's castle, Ti-Jean put his toad in the stable and took a comb and curried him as best he could.

"Be careful of the king's comb," jeered the other two fellows. "You may break it."

The next morning the three young fellows got up and prepared to meet the king. The king admired the two beautiful horses that the first two young men had brought. "Now Ti-Jean, my fine fellow," he said. "Where is your horse?"

"Oh," the others laughed, "you'll never guess. He actually rode in on a toad."

"A toad," said the king. "Come, come, I must see that for sure."

Ti-Jean went to the stable and came back leading the most magnificent horse anybody had ever seen. Its hooves were gold and its mane was of silver.

"Well, it's obvious," said the king, "that Ti-Jean has won this test, but you know a king always devises three tests. So there are two more to go. Now, whoever brings me the finest homespun will inherit my crown."

Ti-Jean and the other two young men went off down the same road, and when they came to the fork, they each took the same road they had before. Ti-Jean wandered down the long path until he came to the same little thatched house. Again he saw the white cat and four toads filling the tub with water. Ti-Jean watched the white cat and, as she had the day before, when the tub was filled with water she jumped in and emerged the most beautiful princess Ti-Jean had ever seen.

"Hello, there," she said. "Ti-Jean, now what are you looking for?"

"I took the king the most beautiful horse in the world and now he wants the finest homespun ever made, before I can inherit his crown."

"Very well," said the princess. "Tomorrow morning I will turn into a cat again. Go and look in the big chest in the barn and select the ugliest walnut that you can find. Take it with you and when you go before the king, open it with a sharp knife. You will find thirty yards of the finest homespun you have ever seen."

The next day, Ti-Jean selected the ugliest walnut and put

it in his pocket. When he met his two rivals at the crossroads, they laughed and they jeered, for they saw that Ti-Jean had nothing.

At the castle, the first two fellows showed the king the beautiful homespun they had found. Then they said, "That fellow, Ti-Jean, he doesn't have anything to show."

With twinkling eyes, Ti-Jean put his hand in his pocket and brought forth the walnut. He placed it in the king's hand and said, "Take a knife, Your Majesty, cut it open and you shall see what you shall see." The king broke open the walnut, and there flowed forth thirty yards of the finest homespun he had ever seen.

"Ti-Jean wins again, but there is still the third task. This time, whoever brings back the most beautiful princess for a bride will inherit my crown."

They all hurried off down the road again and when they came to the crossroads, each went down the same road as before. Ti-Jean traveled and traveled until he came to the cottage with the straw thatch. There he saw the big white cat carrying water and filling the tub as before. She jumped into the tub and emerged as a beautiful princess. By this time, Ti-Jean had fallen madly in love with her.

"Well, now, Ti-Jean," she said. "What did you come for this time?"

"The king has given me a third task. He says that whoever brings back the most beautiful princess for a bride will inherit his crown. You are the most beautiful girl I've ever seen in my life."

"I turn into a cat every morning, and I can never be a princess again unless a king agrees to marry me."

"That's all right," said Ti-Jean. "You just come with me."

"Tomorrow," she said, "I will turn into a big white cat again. You harness those four toads to the old coach in the stable and we will go together."

The next morning, Ti-Jean found the four toads and harnessed them to the old coach. He placed the white cat in the coach, where she purred contentedly. Then he got up and with a little bit of string, he whipped up the toads and off they traveled down the path.

The other two young men had very nice-looking girls. They looked at Ti-Jean and the white cat and the four toads and they sneered, "Well, the king will take one look and that will be the end of you. Don't follow close to us. We'll be the laughing stock of the village."

Ti-Jean just grinned from ear to ear as he whipped up the toads with his piece of string. Finally they arrived at the castle. Ti-Jean took the toads and the white cat to the stable and he groomed the toads with his comb.

"Ti-Jean," said the other two, "you'll break the king's comb."

"Oh," said Ti-Jean, "it may be my comb soon enough, and then I can do what I want with it."

The next morning, the king admired the beautiful ladies that the two fellows had brought. Then he said, "Now, Ti-Jean, what about you?"

"Oh, Ti-Jean, he's only got a great big white cat to show."

"Nevertheless," said the king, "I must see it."

Ti-Jean went and brought forth the cat. She had turned into a princess. The king was very surprised. She was so beautiful that he couldn't take his eyes off her. Then Ti-Jean went out and brought in the toads, and they were four of the most beautiful horses the king had ever seen.

"Well, Ti-Jean, you are the winner," said the king. He took the crown off his head and placed it on the head of Ti-Jean. Ti-Jean married the beautiful princess and that wedding was celebrated for days, far and near.

NOTES AND ACKNOWLEDGEMENTS

THE FOLKLORE tradition of Canada, unlike that of Oriental or European nations, is relatively new. The French and English settlers who came to Canada in its early stages of development brought with them a rich heritage of stories and songs that had been transmitted down through the generations of their families. The stories teemed with the giants, mischief-makers, simpletons, princes, princesses and mysterious beasts that were familiar characters in the stories of the Grimm Brothers. Good and evil spirits and the fear of the unknown were always present. Because of the isolation of the early Canadian communities many of the stories have retained the purity of their original roots.

The stories in this collection have been adapted from both French- and English-Canadian sources. Most of the stories were collected by folklorists in the early twentieth century from the second or third generations of settlers who in their retelling of the stories retained the original theme motifs, and adapted the stories to suit their new environment. One of the most significant features of all of these stories is the dominant presence of the forest, a forest that was deep and mysterious and where strange and fearsome creatures prowled and were a constant threat to the well-being of the settlers.

The only indigenous folktales of Canada belong to the native Canadian Indian and Inuit peoples. Because these native peoples have such a unique and beautiful tradition of storytelling, no attempt has been made to adapt their stories for this collection. Too often English-speaking storytellers retell native tales only from their own perspective, imposing upon the tales their own vision of life.

The adaptation of tales for this collection has been made for the children of the eighties, in the spirit expressed by the Italian storyteller, Italo Calvino — "The tale is not beautiful if nothing is added. Folktales remain merely dumb until you realize that you are required to complete them yourself, to fill in your own particulars."

The tales in this book have been adapted from the following sources:

The Healing Spring. Fauset, Arthur. "Folklore from Nova Scotia," in: *Memoirs of the American Folk-lore Society.* American Folk-lore Society, 1913.

NOTES AND ACKNOWLEDGEMENTS

The Princess of Tomboso. Barbeau, Marius. "La Princesse du Tomboso," in: *Contes de Charlevoix et de Chicoutimi.* The Journal of American Folk-lore, Vol. 32, Book 123, 1919.

The Three Golden Hairs. Spray, Carole. *Will o' the wisp; folk tales and legends of New Brunswick.* Brunswick Press, 1979.

Little Golden Sun and Little Golden Star. Lemieux, Germain. "Le petite soleil — et la petite étoile d'or," in: *Les vieux m'ont conté.* Centre Franco-Ontarien de Folklore, Université de Sudbury, 1974.

The Fairy Child. Fraser, Mary. *Folklore of Nova Scotia.* Formac, 1975.

Petit Jean and the Witch. Barbeau, Marius. "Cheveux d'or," in: *Les contes du grand-père sept-heures.* Les éditions chantecler, n.d.

Goldenhair. Barbeau, Marius. "Cheveux d'or," in: *Les contes du grand-père sept-heures.* Les éditions chantecler, n.d.

St. Nicholas and the Children. Macmillan, Cyrus. *Canadian wonder tales.* Bodley Head (Canada) and Clarke Irwin, 1974.

Beauty and the Beast. Lemieux, Germain. "La Belle et la bête," in: *Les vieux m'ont conté.* Centre Franco-Ontarien de Folklore, Université de Sudbury, 1974.

Ti-Jean and the Unicorn. Wallace, Paul A., ed. *Baptiste Larocque: Legends of French Canada.* Musson, 1923.

Ti-Jean Brings Home the Moon. Wallace, Paul A., ed. *Baptiste Larocque: Legends of French Canada.* Musson, 1923.

Ti-Jean and the White Cat. Wallace, Paul A., ed. *Baptiste Larocque: Legends of French Canada.* Musson, 1923.